Come and Play, Hippo

An I Can Read Book®

Come and Play, Hippo

by Mike Thaler
pictures by Maxie Chambliss

HarperTrophy

A Division of HarperCollinsPublishers

Come and Play, Hippo
Text copyright © 1991 by Mike Thaler
Illustrations copyright © 1991 by Maxie Chambliss
Printed in the U.S.A. All rights reserved.
First Harper Trophy edition, 1993.

Library of Congress Cataloging-in-Publication Data
Thaler, Mike, date
    Come and play, hippo / by Mike Thaler ; pictures by Maxie Chambliss.—
1st ed.
        p.   cm. — (An I can read book)
    Summary: In four stories about Hippo and his jungle friends, Snake latches
onto Hippo, the animals are vexed by Friday the 13th, Hippo starts a band,
and Hippo makes magic.
    ISBN 0-06-026176-5. — ISBN 0-06-026177-3 (lib. bdg.)
    ISBN 0-06-444165-2 (pbk.)
    [1. Hippopotamus—Fiction.   2. Jungle animals—Fiction.   3. Animals—
Fiction.]   I. Chambliss, Maxie, ill.   II. Title.   III. Series.
PZ7.T3CON   1991   87-33489
[E]—dc19   CIP
                                                                       AC

For Andrea Brown—
Up Front In Work
And My Heart
　　　　—M.T.

To Miss Sweet's wonderful
first-grade class.
　　　　—M.C.

Contents

Snake Stockings

"What would you like to play today?"
asked Hippo.

"Let's play BOA CONSTRICTOR,"
said Snake.

"How do you play that?"
asked Hippo.

"I wrap myself around your leg
and don't let go."

"That doesn't sound like fun,"
said Hippo.

"Oh, it is," said Snake.

"I'll show you."

He wrapped himself
around Hippo's leg.

"There. Isn't this fun?"

"No," said Hippo.

"I am having fun," said Snake.

"I am leaving," said Hippo.

Hippo shook his leg.

Snake was still on it.

Snake smiled. "FUN!"

"Get off my leg," said Hippo.

"No," said Snake.

"Get off my leg!" shouted Hippo,

jumping up and down.

"What FUN!" said Snake.

13

Hippo sat down on a log.

Just then Mole came by.

"That's a nice stocking,"

said Mole.

"That is not a stocking,"
said Hippo.

"That is a snake."
Mole looked closer.
Snake smiled.

"Why are you on his leg?"
asked Mole.

"We are playing," said Snake.

"Can I play too?" asked Mole.

"Sure," said Snake.

"Just grab his other leg
and hold tight."
Mole grabbed Hippo's other leg.

"This is crazy," said Hippo.

He stood up

and wiggled his legs.

"Fun!" cried Mole.

"FUN!" said Snake.

16

"Why are you dancing?" asked Lion.

"I am not dancing," said Hippo.

"I will dance with you!" said Lion, and he took Hippo's hand.

"I will dance too!"

yelled Elephant.

He grabbed Hippo's other hand

and wiggled his bottom.

Hippo looked at Elephant

and laughed.

"Fun!" said Hippo.

And that's the way

he spent the day—

with his arms dancing,

and his feet at play.

Friday the Thirteenth

Hippo skipped to Mole's hole.

"Mole," he shouted.

"Come and play!"

Mole stuck his head out slowly.

He looked around.

"Not today," he said.

"Why not today?" shouted Hippo.

Mole looked around.

"It is Friday the thirteenth,"

he said.

"So?" shouted Hippo.

"It's unlucky!" said Mole.

"Big deal!" Hippo giggled.

"There is nothing to worry about."

Mole looked around.

"It *is* unlucky," he said.

"Don't be silly," said Hippo.

He stood up and danced around.

He did not see Monkey's banana peel.

SLIP! WHOOSH! WHAM!

Hippo was lying on his back.

"See!" said Mole.

Hippo looked up at the sky
and smiled.

"It was just an accident," he said,
and brushed himself off.

23

"Come out, and I will show you

there is nothing to worry about."

Slowly Mole came out of his hole.

"Come on!" said Hippo.

He took Mole's paw.

Mole looked around.

They started off into the jungle.

But Hippo did not see

the log in the road.

WHUMP! WHOOSH! WHAM!

Hippo was lying on his stomach

with his nose in the leaves.

24

"See!" said Mole.

Hippo smiled.

"Just an accident,"

he said,

and brushed the leaves off his nose.

25

Hippo stood up.

He did not see

the low-hanging branch.

BUMP! WHAM!

Hippo was back on the ground.

"Friday the thirteenth," said Mole.

"Nonsense!" said Hippo.

Just then

a coconut dropped from a tree.

BUMP! WHUMP!

Hippo was back on the ground.

"Well," said Mole,

"I guess you are right.

There *is* nothing to worry about.

Let's play."

Hippo looked around.

He rubbed his head.

"I think I am going home,"

he said.

And he did not get out of the river

until Saturday the fourteenth.

Hippo Starts a Band

One morning Hippo decided
to start a band.
He ran to tell Monkey.
Monkey thought it was a great idea.
They ran to tell Snake.
Snake loved the idea too,
so they ran to tell Giraffe.

Giraffe thought

it was the best idea

he had heard all day.

So they ran to tell

Lion and Elephant.

Soon they were all together.

"What do we do first?"

asked Snake.

"First," said Hippo,

"we each pick an instrument."

"I want to play the trumpet," said Elephant.

"I want to play the trumpet too," said Lion.

"I like the trumpet also," said Giraffe.

"A trumpet for me," said Snake.

"I want to play the piano," said Monkey.

33

"Wait a minute," said Hippo,
"this is a marching band.
A marching band
cannot have a piano.
Besides, you have to pick
different instruments."

"But I will play
the trumpet," said Elephant.

"Okay," said Giraffe,
"I will play the trombone."

"Then I will play
the flute," said Lion.

"I will play
the clarinet," said Snake.

"And I will play the piano,"
said Monkey.

35

"You cannot play the piano,"
said Hippo.
"If I cannot play the piano,
then I will not play at all,"
said Monkey.
"What about the drum?" said Lion.
"Okay," said Monkey.
"I will play the drum."
They all ran to the music store
and got their instruments
and their band caps.
Hippo got a whistle,
and they went back to the jungle.

They made a terrible lot of noise.

Hippo blew his whistle.

"We have to pick a song," he said.

"I like 'Jungle Bells,'" said Elephant,

and he started to play it.

"I like 'Jungle Bridges Falling Down,'"

said Giraffe,

and he started to play *that*.

"I like 'Wiggle, Wiggle, Wiggle,'"

said Snake,

and he started to play *that*.

Monkey started to jump up and down

on his drum.

Lion began to roar.

Hippo blew his whistle.

"We have to play the *same* song."

"How does it go?" asked Monkey.

"The *same song*!" shouted Hippo.

"What about 'Hold That Tiger'?"
asked Lion.

They all began to play
"Hold That Tiger."

41

Hippo blew his whistle, loud.

"What's the matter now?" asked Snake.

"You all have to play

in the *same* key," said Hippo.

"I don't know that song," said Monkey.

"Can you hum it?"

"In the *key of C*!" shouted Hippo.

So they all played

in the same key.

Elephant finished first.

Snake finished second.

Giraffe finished third.

Lion finished fourth.

Monkey didn't finish

until Hippo blew his whistle.

44

"I won,"

said Elephant.

"Wait a minute," said Hippo.

"You have to play *together*."

"I never heard that one,"

said Monkey.

"Together!!" shouted Hippo.

So they all played together.

"That is beautiful," said Hippo.

A tear came to his eye.

"Now we have to march."

"Can't we just sit?" asked Elephant.

"No!" said Hippo.

"We are a *marching* band."

So they all lined up.

Hippo blew his whistle.

They all started marching.

Monkey marched into a tree.

Lion marched into the bushes.

Snake marched into Giraffe.

And Elephant marched into the river.

Hippo blew his whistle.

They all lined up again.

"We have to march *together*,"

said Hippo.

Hippo blew his whistle.

And they marched

and played

all day.

Hippo Makes Magic

"Today I would like to make magic,"

said Hippo.

He put on

his new magician's hat and cape.

He picked up

seven pieces of paper and a pencil.

"I will now turn these blank
pieces of paper into signs."
And he did.

The signs said:

Magic Show
at River's Edge
Twelve noon

He put the signs

all over the jungle.

At noon all his friends

were seated by the river.

Hippo stood in front of them.

"This should be good,"

said Snake, and he poked Lion.

"For my first and only trick,"

said Hippo,

"I will make the sun

disappear from the sky."

Hippo threw back his cape

and raised both arms.

"Abra Cadabra Cadoodle!"

His friends looked up.

The sun was still there.

"This trick may take a little time,"

said Hippo.

At one o'clock they all had lunch.

At two o'clock they rested.

At three o'clock they sang songs.

At four o'clock they played games.

At five o'clock

they danced around in a circle.

And at six o'clock

the sun disappeared

from the sky.

They all clapped in the dark.

Hippo bowed.

"Gee," said Snake.

"How did you do it?"

"Well," said Hippo,

taking off his hat,

"it just takes a little patience

and good friends."